S0-EDC-728

Copyright © 2015 | Joslynn Jarrett-Skelton

All rights reserved. No part of this book may be reproduced or transmitted in any form or by any means, electronic or mechanical, including photocopying, recording, or by any information storage and retrieval system, without written permission from the publisher.

Printed in the United States of America. For information address Hearts For Charlie, PO Box 2812, Pismo Beach CA, 93448

Library of Congress Cataloging-in-Publication Data

Paperback ISBN 978-0-9965362-0-2

Hearts for Charlie books are available for special promotions and premiums. For details contact Joslynn Skelton, Author of Charlie the Courageous PO Box 2812, Pismo Beach CA 93448

First paperback edition
Printed in PRC

Visit Us at www.heartsforcharlie.com

Editing and Publishing Consulting by Jack San Filippo
Layout and Print Consulting by James Morgan
Book Design by Andrew Skelton

Charlie

the Courageous

Joslynn Jarrett-Skelton

Illustrated by Adam Walker-Parker

Dedicated to:

The amazing staff at Children's Hospital Los Angeles, for loving our Charlie as if she was your own.

To Dr. Herrington, Dr. Votava-Smith and Dr. Ing, for mending our Charlie's heart time and time again.

To our family, who have loved us unconditionally, stood beside us, and were there for us in whatever form we needed you to be.

And to our little Charlie, for being courageous enough to inspire this book in the first place.

There once was a little girl named Charlie.
She was born blue, but darling.

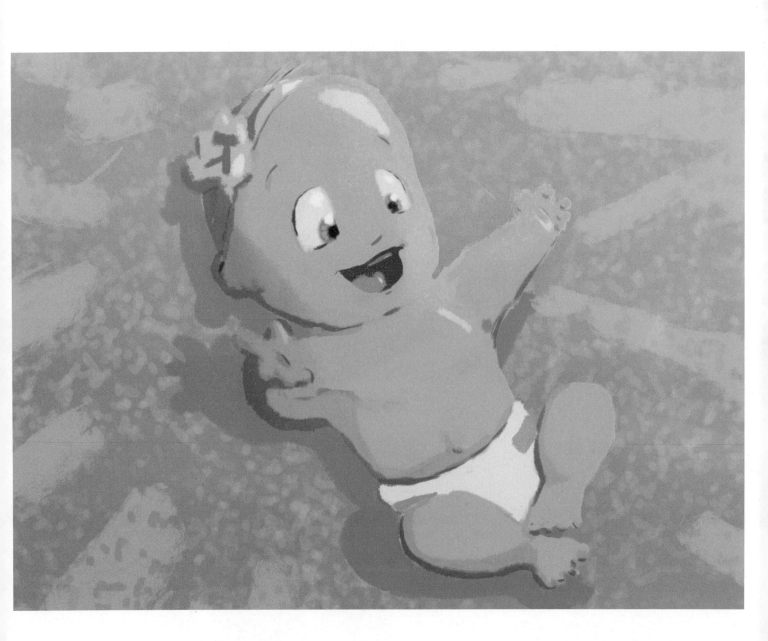

The doctors had to
take her away...

...so they could
mend her heart
that day.

She grew up with super powers, but only she knew,
how courageous and brave she was
through and through.

So on her adventures she would go,
with her sisters both in tow.

To help other children,
and be true.
To show them their inner
beauty and that they,
can be super heroes too.

So with her cape, mask, and mighty heart scar...
She set out to find children both near and far.

Then off to the park she
went one summer day...
Charlie with her sisters,
Makayla and Sawyer,
all set out to play.

There were children everywhere playing tag, but Charlie knew it would be hard for her to keep up, to zig and to zag.

Even though she tried hard to run away,

Charlie kept getting tagged and could hardly play.

With her sisters by her side,
she told the kids her story.

All about her unique heart and giving God all the glory.

So all the children decided to play a little slower.
To help Charlie out so she wouldn't get run over.
Teaching the kids that everyone can be included,
because it's no fun being the one kid who's excluded.

For all of us are different, in our own special ways,
but we should all love each other anyway.

Charlie the Courageous she will be called
and through her adventures,
she will get to know you all.

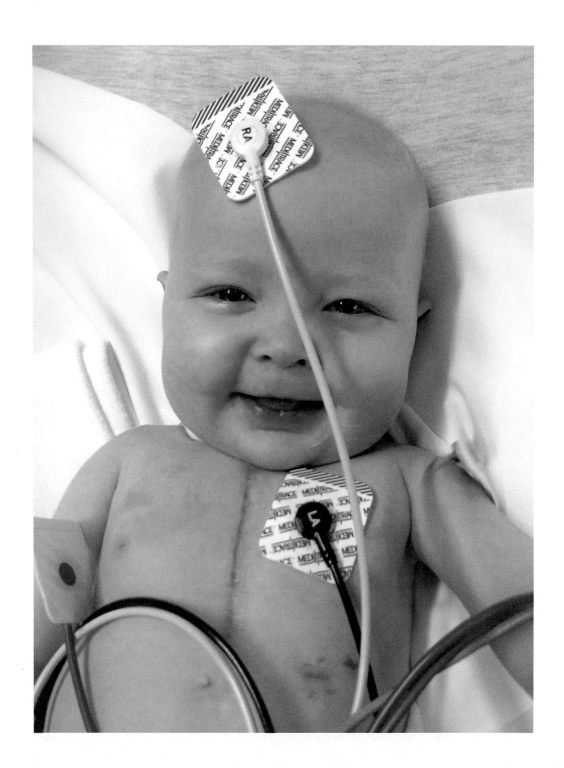

Charlie was born missing the left side of her heart, and within her first week of life underwent her first of three lifesaving open-heart surgeries. As the youngest of three sisters, and eight grandchildren, our whole family came together to support Charlie and get her through the roughest year of her life. It was through this journey that we learned that 1 out of 100 babies are born with a congenital heart defect and it is the number 1 killer of infants and children, yet it is one of the least funded of all childhood maladies. During her second open-heart surgery, we happened to be in the hospital over Thanksgiving. While sitting on the cardiac floor of Children's Hospital Los Angeles with so many children and their families, I realized that these kids need someone to relate to, they need someone who they can look to and not feel alone. This is when Charlie the Courageous was born! Not only is this book meant to bring hope and inspiration to families going through any kind of life threatening diagnoses, but it is also meant to bring awareness to congenital heart defects and teach children how to embrace each other's differences, whatever they may be. For a child missing half of her heart, she has brought more heart and love to our family than we could have ever expected. Although our journey may get scary at times, we choose to see the beauty of this path that we have been led down.

Yes to Your will, yes to Your ways, we lift up our hands and say, "YES!!"

The Skelton Family,
Andrew, Joslynn, Makayla, Sawyer,
and our little Charlie the Courageous!

Follow Charlie's journey at www.heartsforcharlie.com

Stay Tuned for Book #2:
Charlie the Courageous, Love for Lawson.
Coming Soon!

For every book purchased, a book is donated to a child fighting a CHD.